# It's All Relative!

Adapted by Sarah Nathan

Based on the series created by Todd J. Greenwald

Part One is based on the episode, "You Can't Always Get What You Carpet," Written by Peter Murrieta

Part Two is based on the episode, "Crazy 10 Minute Sale," Written by Todd J. Greenwald

**New York**

AN IMPRINT OF DISNEY BOOK GROUP

Copyright © 2008 Disney Enterprises, Inc.

All rights reserved. Published by Disney Press, an imprint of Disney Book Group.
No part of this book may be reproduced or transmitted in any form or by any
means, electronic or mechanical, including photocopying, recording,
or by any information storage and retrieval system, without
written permission from the publisher. For information address
Disney Press, 114 Fifth Avenue, New York, New York 10011-5690.

Printed in the United States of America

First Edition
1 3 5 7 9 10 8 6 4 2

Library of Congress Catalog Card Number: 2007942959
ISBN 978-1-4231-1289-1

For more Disney Press fun, visit www.disneybooks.com
Visit DisneyChannel.com

If you purchased this book without a cover, you should be aware
that this book is stolen property. It was reported as "unsold and
destroyed" to the publisher, and neither the author nor the
publisher has received any payment for this "stripped" book.

# PART ONE

# Chapter One

Justin Russo and his younger brother, Max, were hard at work. With tool belts strapped around their waists, they were helping their dad remodel their sister Alex's room. While Alex was out shopping, they were hanging new wallpaper and giving the room a makeover. Jerry Russo, the boys' father, stood proudly, admiring their work.

"Alex is going to love her room!" Mr. Russo exclaimed as he looked up at the one completed wall. He pointed to the colorful wallpaper. "The flowery thingies are perfect for my little princess."

Max wasn't paying attention. He was more interested in looking at the superstrength glue on his fingers than at the wallpaper. "Hey, check it out," he said, holding up his hand. "The wallpaper glue dried my fingers together." On the worktable in front of him was a square piece of wood. He positioned himself like a black-belt master with his hand poised for a karate chop. "Hiya!" he yelled, as he slammed his hand against the wooden plank.

"Dude, that's awesome!" Justin exclaimed. "Give it up." He held up his hand to hit a high five with Max. But the wood stuck to Max's hand and accidentally hit Justin's hand. "Ow!" Justin cried.

"Come on, guys, stop messing around, all right?" their father pleaded. He was assessing the task at hand. "To do this job right, you need to focus, you need intensity . . ." He lost his train of thought as he looked down at his tool belt. Stuck in one of the pockets of the belt was a can of soda. ". . . and a root beer," he added, as he took a huge sip.

Just then, Alex walked into the room, carrying two large shopping bags. "Hi, Daddy," she said, doing a quick check of the progress of her room renovation. "I like the new wallpaper," she said, nodding her head. But then she quickly added, "And I'm glad you're not finished yet, because you're really going to love this." From her bag, she pulled out a sample roll of wallpaper and handed it to her dad with a huge smile. "Pink fur wallpaper!" she exclaimed.

"Uh-oh," Max moaned.

Justin rolled his eyes. He had seen this act before. Alex getting what she wanted was something he'd witnessed many times. Sure, all the Russo kids had magical powers, but Alex's power over their dad was mystifying to both Justin and Max. All three kids were wizards in training and could perform magic—but only in secret. No one knew that they were wizards, especially not kids at school or the customers who ate in the Waverly Place Sub Station, the restaurant that the family owns and runs, which is right downstairs from their apartment. The restaurant is located in the heart of Greenwich Village, and is always packed with students or shoppers who drop in to have a quick bite.

Every Tuesday and Thursday the Russo kids have magic lessons in their basement, which is a secret lair filled with potions, crystal balls, and books of spells. Although their dad taught them their magical skills, he had no actual magic powers himself. He had given them up when he married a mortal—their mom. Their mom knew all about the Russo powers, but she tried to keep their magical skills to a minimum so they could just be normal kids. But Alex seemed to be able to get their dad to do exactly what she wanted—*without* even using wizard magic.

Justin leaned over to Max. "Watch Daddy's little girl make us put up her new wall . . . fur," he mumbled.

Alex was too excited about her new wallpaper to be distracted by her brothers. "Don't you love it?" Alex asked, stroking the piece of fuzzy pink fur.

"What, uh . . . but what about the little flowers?" her father asked, trying to bring her focus back to her original choice.

"It's a little young for me," Alex told him. She pointed to the fur. "I think I'm ready for *this*." She moved closer to her dad. "I almost didn't get the pink fur because the guy at the store said only a professional could put it up." She flashed her dad a smile. "But he doesn't know my daaa-ad!" she sang.

"Well, you got that right," Mr. Russo said, flattered. "The Russo boys are on it!" He turned to his sons. "We're gonna need more glue."

"Yeah, but I thought we were going to work on my room next," Justin complained.

"Your room's good enough," his dad said, gathering up the equipment in the room.

"Good enough for Justin's room, maybe, not for the *J Man*," Justin balked. He did a little strut across the floor.

Max held up his hand. "Wha—Who's the *J Man*?" he asked, clearly confused.

Justin pointed to himself. "Me. That's my nickname."

Laughing, Max said, "Yeah, who calls you that?"

Justin picked up a large container of glue and started to stir quickly. "Lots of people. You know, not at school, but around the neighborhood," he said. Then he saw Max's look of disbelief. "Okay, a couple. Me mostly. But that's just because we haven't redone my room."

Mr. Russo looked over at Justin and grabbed the glue. "Your room looks great."

"No, Justin's right," Alex cooed. "We shouldn't forget about him." She gave him a sly smile. "That's why he should have *this* wallpaper." She pointed to the flowery print.

Quickly, Justin dismissed that idea. "I'm comfortable being forgotten," he said, trying to sound convincing.

"It will totally tie together your little action figures and the big water stain from where the roof leaks," Alex taunted, egging him on.

"I was going to paint over that water stain, but you know what? No, you're right. This wallpaper would look way better," Justin said, his voice dripping with sarcasm.

Unfortunately, his dad didn't get that he was kidding. "Attaboy," he said, patting Justin on the back. "Come on, guys. Let's go before it dries. Fun and games are over." And with that, Mr. Russo was gone, ready to start the new wallpaper project.

"Dad, I was kidding!" Justin called after him. But it was too late. He turned to his sister. "You've got to show me how you do that."

"Unless you want to be Daddy's little girl, I can't help you," she told him, giving him a satisfied grin. She walked out of the room.

Justin sighed. If he was going to be stuck with flowery wallpaper in his room, he'd have to find some new decorations to make it look like a room fit for the *J Man*. Alex wasn't the only one who was going to do some remodeling. He had to get on that—and quick!

# Chapter Two

Later that day, Theresa Russo was busy preparing dinner when Alex walked into the kitchen. She looked up to see her daughter lugging a huge, rolled-up carpet into the room.

"Honey, you didn't make a giant burrito out of Max again, did you?" her mom asked curiously. She rushed over to check inside the rolled carpet.

"No, Mom, it's no fun anymore," Alex admitted. "He likes it." She nodded to the

**11**

carpet in her arms. "The rug's for my room. I found it in the basement."

Lowering her voice, her mother leaned closer to her. "Honey, you know you're not supposed to be going down there."

"Well, Daddy said I could take whatever I want from down there," Alex reported.

Her mother sighed. "Oh, well, all right." Alex always knew exactly how to get her way with her father.

Alex headed up the stairs, dragging the carpet behind her. She knew it would look just perfect with her new wallpaper.

Just then, Max and Justin walked into the kitchen. They were covered in pink fur!

Mrs. Russo looked at her sons and gasped. "Oh, my gosh, what happened to you guys?"

"What happened was Alex got pink fur wallpaper and we just finished hanging it up for her," Max grumbled.

Justin stepped forward. "Mom, will you

vacuum us off?" He handed her the vacuum attachment, looking nervously at the long nozzle. "Be careful."

Max leaped away from the vacuum cleaner. "I don't want to be vacuumed. I'm wearing this to school tomorrow," he said, puffing out his chest. He dashed up the stairs before his mom could clean him up.

Mrs. Russo laughed and then turned her attention back to making dinner. Justin took a seat at the counter in front of her. Welcoming the chance to talk, she looked over at him. "So, Justin, how's your room coming along?" she asked.

"I have girl wallpaper," he complained.

Not sure how to react, his mom asked, "And are you okay with that?"

"No!" Justin cried. "I've got to make it a man's room. I need man stuff."

Stirring the stew in the pot on the stove, his mother inquired some more. "Okay, like what?"

Justin thought for a moment. He thought of the manliest things he could. "Like . . . pictures of girls on motorcycles and my favorite band, Tears of Blood."

"Listen, that sounds awesome, and like I'll probably not be visiting your room that often," his mom joked. She leaned in closer to him. "But if you want some real scary stuff, Dad's chair shaped like a baseball glove . . . it's in the basement."

"Oh, that's awesome!" Justin exclaimed, leaping off the stool. He headed for the basement door.

Just at that moment, Mr. Russo came racing down the stairs. "Baseball-glove chair? Whoo-hoo!" he cheered. He grinned at his wife. "I knew you didn't throw it away. I can't wait to sit in it!" He followed Justin down the stairs.

Meanwhile, in her room, Alex was admiring how her new rug looked with the pink fur walls. She carefully smoothed out the carpet and then grabbed a brush. But instead of brushing her hair—she brushed the furry wall. My room is so cool, she thought happily.

Stretching up to reach as high as she could, Alex soon realized that she was moving up higher and higher toward the ceiling. She glanced down below and saw that she was well above the ground. She was floating in mid-air with the carpet underneath her!

Back in the kitchen, Mrs. Russo was busy pulling a large wad of pink fur from her husband's ear. "Ew!" she cried when she saw the fur ball.

"Ahh," Mr. Russo sighed. He was quite relieved to have that out of his ear.

Checking to see that his ears were all clear, Mrs. Russo gave him a tap on his shoulder. "That's it, honey. You're good," she said.

Mr. Russo fell back into the chair behind

him. "Fits like a glove," he said. Then he laughed to himself as he rubbed his hands on the leather chair. "Hey, it is!" He grinned as he snuggled down in his old chair.

"Listen, that's going in Justin's room," Mrs. Russo warned.

"But—" Mr. Russo started to protest.

Just then, Justin opened the door. "Guys, check it out!" he called. He held up more treasures that he had found stored in the basement. "This tiki dude's going to man up my room. And so is the guitar, after I smash it and hang it on the wall."

His mom grabbed the guitar out of his hands. "You're not smashing anything! That's mine. I used to play it in an all-girl mariachi band at Las Pinatas." She squealed in delight and started to strum the guitar.

His dad rolled his eyes, acknowledging his wife's off-key notes. He grabbed the neck of the guitar to silence his wife's strumming.

"Thanks for finding it," he said sarcastically to his son.

"No, honey, thank *you*," Mrs. Russo said, turning to her husband. "If you hadn't sent Alex down there to get that rug, we never would've found it."

Mr. Russo was stunned. "Wha—hold on, what rug?"

*CRASH!*

They all looked up. The sound came from Alex's room.

"Alex?" her mom called out nervously.

They ran up to Alex's room. But she was nowhere to be found.

"Honey?" her dad asked, looking around.

"Alex?" Mrs. Russo called again, still clutching her guitar.

"I thought she had the magic flying carpet," Mr. Russo said with a sigh of relief. But he didn't stay relaxed for long.

Just then, Alex tumbled down, falling flat

on her face in front of her parents and Justin! She grunted as she landed with a thud.

Her mother gasped. There were bits of the ceiling falling all around the room.

Alex quickly stood up to show that she wasn't hurt. She tried to act natural—as if she hadn't just fallen through the roof. "Hey. So, how's it going?" she said, acting supercasual. "Mom, I see you have the guitar out. You thinking about playing it now?"

Her dad stepped closer to her. "Alex, stop trying to avoid the subject," he ordered.

"Daddy, you said I could take stuff from the basement," Alex argued.

Her mother scolded her. "You know you're not supposed to use magic unsupervised."

"You should've come to me as soon as you realized that was a magic carpet," her dad said sternly.

"Daddy, I really didn't do anything wrong." Alex pleaded her case. She looked innocently at him as she said, "It's not like I was giving people rides."

Suddenly, Max came flying through the large hole in the ceiling. "Woo-hoo!" he cheered as he bounced up off the floor. He shook the plaster out of his hair and looked over at his sister. "Can I go again?"

Alex quickly noticed her parents' disapproving faces. She was busted. Not only did she crash through the ceiling on a flying carpet—she was giving her little brother a joy ride. Flying a carpet without lessons was strictly forbidden. She was in trouble. *Big* trouble.

# Chapter Three

Mrs. Russo did not waste another minute. She quickly rolled up the old carpet and threw it over her shoulder. "That's it," she said as she carried it out of the room. "I'm taking this carpet right back to the basement."

As she left, Mr. Russo called after her. "And why don't you leave your guitar down there, too, honey!"

She turned around. "Listen, if your baseball-glove chair stays above ground, so does my guitar," she said as she left the room.

Mr. Russo walked over to Alex. "I am really disappointed in you," he said with a frown.

"Daddy, the rug looks great in here!" Alex exclaimed, trying to distract him from the mess around her. "It ties the whole room together."

Mr. Russo waved his hand at the pile of plaster on the floor. "Look around you. I can't let you keep a magic carpet. You don't even know how to drive it."

Attempting to capitalize on the moment, Alex pushed the issue with her dad. "So you should teach me how to drive the carpet," she said sweetly, trying to convince him.

Shaking his head, her father was adamant. "No way."

Justin stood by the door with Max. He was shocked. "I can't believe it," he whispered to Max. "He just said no—to Daddy's little girl!"

Mr. Russo ignored his son's comment. "Absolutely not," he told Alex. "And don't

21

look at me with those puppy-dog eyes and think I'm just going to melt in your hands."

"Is that what you think I do, Daddy?" Alex shrugged and gave him her best defeated look. "Okay."

Her dad paused. "No, no, no, no, *no*," he told her. "You are *not* going to guilt me into this." He tried to remain firm. He looked over at his sons standing in the doorway. "Uh, just because I taught Justin, doesn't mean I automatically have to . . ." As soon as the words left his mouth, he realized what he had just confessed. "Uh-oh," he groaned.

"You taught Justin?" Alex exclaimed in surprise. She was not going to let her dad get away with that! She took a position that she knew would win him over. "Well, I guess that makes sense, since he's your firstborn, and he'll always have a more special place in your heart than me." She sat down on her bed to sulk.

"Oh, you can't possibly think that I love

him more than you," her dad argued. He pointed to his sons. "I love you all equally." He started to walk out the door. "We'll talk about this in the morning. Good night."

"It's only four o'clock," Justin noted.

Mr. Russo turned and shot Justin an exasperated look. "Who are you? Father Time?"

"Daddy, give me one good reason why I can't learn how to fly the carpet," Alex whined as she stood up.

"You can't fly the carpet because you're not old enough," he said flatly.

There was no way Alex was going to let her dad off the hook so quickly. "Well, how old was Justin?" she pressed him.

"Eighteen," Mr. Russo said.

Justin looked at his dad in confusion. "I'm sixteen now."

"Oh, so you lied to me, huh?" his dad bellowed. He headed toward the door. "Well, we'll talk about that in the morning. Good night!" He stormed out of the room.

"Okay, Daddy," Alex said, following her dad out into the hallway. "Even though you haven't given me a good reason, I know you must have one, because . . ." Alex paused and placed her hand lovingly on her dad's shoulder. ". . . that's how much I respect you and love you."

Mr. Russo couldn't resist Alex's charm. He sighed. "Okay. Fine," he finally agreed. "We'll start carpet-flying lessons tomorrow."

Smirking, Alex strutted back into her room.

"And that's how you do *that*," she said, grinning at her brothers, who stared at her in disbelief.

Once again, Alex had worked her magic on her dad. And now she was going to get flying lessons. Perfect.

# Chapter Four

The next evening, Alex was really excited. She couldn't wait for her flying lessons to begin! She watched her dad as he fiddled with the magic carpet's engine. They were both wearing bright yellow airplane life vests and bicycle helmets in anticipation of their carpet flight. After a thorough check, Mr. Russo finally finished checking the engine. "And if you don't vacuum it every three thousand miles," her dad explained to her, "the filter gets clogged. It makes for a very unstable ride. Not safe."

Alex shrugged. She wasn't really interested in the inner mechanics of the carpet. She was more focused on the actual driving. "Oh, so I get it. Just bring it to you every three thousand miles so you can do all that stuff, because you're so good at it," she joked.

Mr. Russo chuckled. "Eh, well, it does relax me," he confessed. "Okay, moving on to the rules of the sky. What kind of cloud should you fly into?" He looked over at Alex. "Trick question. None of them! Because it's very easy to become confused in a cloud."

Alex just stared at her dad in bewilderment.

"Which way's up? Which way's down?" he continued. "I don't know. Crash!" He clapped his hands together to emphasize the noise.

Alex looked at her father curiously. "What would you crash into in a cloud?" she asked.

"A confused wizard on a carpet going the other way," her father replied. "Plus, you don't want to expose fine wool to that kind of moisture. It's very hard to dry and then it starts to smell like a camel."

"Is that bad?" Alex asked.

Shaking his head, Mr. Russo said, "You don't want to know."

"Dad," Alex pleaded. "Stop trying to scare me. I'm a big girl. I can handle this."

"You're a big girl, huh?" Mr. Russo said. "Okay, big girl. Enough talk, let's walk. Let's take her up."

"Great, I'm ready!" Alex exclaimed excitedly.

"It's very easy to fly," her dad explained. "All you have to do is curl left, lean right, go left. Curl right, lean left, go right. Curl down, go down. Got it?"

Trying to follow those instructions, Alex repeated, "Curl what, lean who, go where?" She sighed. "Just go slower."

"Go slower?" Mr. Russo asked. "All right, enough chitchat. You don't learn by teaching.

You learn by doing. Let's take her up." He reached over and pulled the cords on Alex's vest to inflate it. "Let's go!"

With a flourish, they sat on the front edge of the carpet and took off. Alex's hands were tightly gripping the fringe of the carpet as they sailed up over Manhattan.

"Hey, isn't this fun?" Alex exclaimed to her dad. Now that they were up in the air, she was really enjoying herself. She looked over at him and smiled. "Just the two of us."

"Why are you looking at me?" her dad scolded. "Eyes on the sky—not me, the sky! Honey, come on."

But Alex was too busy looking at the sights around her to really pay attention. Mr. Russo took a deep breath. Alex wasn't listening to his directions at all. "All right, let's turn left . . . here. No, it's too jerky, too jerky. It's all in the wrist. I told you it's in the wrist." He was starting to lose his patience.

Alex was beginning to get frustrated too. Why was her dad being so impatient? she wondered. She was trying to concentrate on all of his directions.

"Look, you're thinking too much!" he exclaimed. "Don't think. Just . . . fly!"

"How can I think when you're yelling?" Alex argued. This lesson was not going the way she had envisioned it. Even though the city skyline was amazing, Alex couldn't enjoy the view—or the ride.

"I'm not yelling. I'm just loud teaching," he explained. All of a sudden, the very tall Chrysler Building, with its sharp steeple, appeared. "Watch out! Watch out!" he cried.

Alex held on to the edge of the carpet tightly. "Watch where? Watch where?" she shouted, looking around.

"Where? Everywhere!" Mr. Russo exclaimed. "Watch everywhere!"

"How can I watch everywhere?" Alex asked in confusion.

At that moment, they almost flew into the Chrysler Building, barely missing the top. "Whoooaaa!" they both screamed.

Alex slowly exhaled. That was a close call. Carpet-flying lessons with her dad were totally not what she expected at all . . . and neither was flying. It was hard work—and a little scary!

Mrs. Russo sat in the living room, strumming her guitar and singing, as she waited for her husband and Alex to return home from their flying lesson. When she saw Alex walk through the patio door, she stopped playing. "Oh, hi, how'd it go?" she asked enthusiastically.

Alex didn't respond. She walked right past her mother to the stairs. "I'm not talking to him!" she declared.

Mr. Russo walked through the terrace doors. He was holding a broken satellite dish in his hands. "I'm not talking to her," he said to his wife. "*Or* watching the big fight tonight," he added glumly, placing a piece of the satellite dish on the kitchen counter.

"No, apparently I am," Mrs. Russo said with a heavy sigh as she watched Alex stomp up the stairs.

Exasperated, Mr. Russo began to explain. "She's not ready for lessons. I don't know why she's so anxious to fly anyway. She needs to be home with us." While he ranted, he searched the refrigerator for a snack. "And where are my pudding cups?"

"You ate them all, remember?" Mrs. Russo gently reminded him.

Still frustrated from his flying experience with Alex, he continued. "Where does she think she's going to on that carpet anyway?"

"I don't know, but wherever it is, honey,

she's going to come back." She lowered her voice. "Sweetie, do you think maybe you're not upset about the flying lessons as much as you are about not wanting our little girl to grow up?"

"That's ridiculous!" Mr. Russo barked. "And until we solve this pudding crisis, I can't even think straight." He walked out of the room with a huff.

Mrs. Russo shook her head. She picked up her pen and grabbed her grocery list. "Need more pudding," she said, writing it down.

Just then, Justin charged into the apartment, holding a large stuffed boar head.

"Mom!" he called. "Check out what someone has thrown out!"

"Oh," she said in surprise, taking a look at the large black boar head. "It's hard to imagine someone not wanting that." Then she looked at her son. "Why do you want that?"

"Something's got to take your eye off that

girlie wallpaper," he explained. "And how can you not look at this?" He sat down on the couch just as Alex came bounding down the stairs.

"Um, Dad's not here, right?" she asked, looking around.

"Why?" Justin taunted. "Daddy's little girl doesn't want to see Daddy?"

"Well, that's what I want to talk to you about. When we were on our lesson, Dad got all tense and frustrated, like how he acts when he's around you and your dolls," she said.

Looking up at his sister, Justin clarified. "Action figures. Collectibles . . . in their original packaging."

"Dad's never acted that way with me before," Alex said softly. She sat down on the couch near Justin. "What should I do about it?"

"I'd love to help, but I've never been Daddy's little favorite anything. That's why I have *girl* wallpaper," Justin told her. Then he looked over at the animal head in his lap. "And I'm hoping that Boris here is going to man that up." He stood up, eager to hang up his new decoration in his room.

"Wait, I really need your help," Alex said. "How do I get Dad to stop being mad at me so he'll teach me how to fly?"

Justin thought for a moment. "What does Dad love even more than pudding?"

A smile spread across Alex's face. "Breakfast for dinner," she answered.

"Exactly," Justin agreed. "You got to make that happen."

"I can do that," Alex said confidently.

"And you've got to get something very special to top it off," Justin coached.

Alex smiled at her brother. She knew exactly what he was thinking. At the same time, they both said, "Baked ziti from Mario's."

Even though it wasn't something that would

be eaten at breakfast, their dad loved it. Alex hoped the combination of two of their dad's favorite things would win him over.

"Yes!" Alex exclaimed. She had a plan. "Now give me ten dollars," she said to Justin.

"What?" Justin asked. "Why?"

"It was your great idea," Alex told him.

Justin shook his head as he handed over the money to his sister. "I can't afford to always be this smart," he quipped.

Alex grinned at her brother. She knew her first flying lesson didn't go exactly as planned, but she hoped her dad would come around. After all, he never could resist her charm. She couldn't wait to see what would happen at dinner . . . or rather, breakfast!

# Chapter Five

When the Russo family sat down for dinner later that evening, there was complete silence at the table. Mr. Russo sat with his arms folded across his chest, ignoring his plate of pancakes. Everyone else was chewing in silence and looking at each other, waiting for the tension to break.

"Dad, um, Mom and I made breakfast for dinner," Alex said, trying to break the silence. "I know it's your favorite."

Mr. Russo ignored Alex and looked at his wife. "Thank you, Theresa."

"Dad, I melted your butter," Alex said, trying again to engage her father in conversation. "And I even went all the way uptown to get that special blueberry syrup you like." She picked up the syrup and poured some onto her dad's plate.

Mr. Russo pushed his plate away. "No thanks," he grumbled. "I'm trying to cut down on fruit."

Seeing an opportunity to add some humor, Max spoke up. "I feel the same way about vegetables. Who's with me?" He looked around the table for some support.

Alex gave Justin a pleading look. Their plan was *so* not working! Justin leaned in and tried to help with the conversation. "And Dad, guess what Alex got you for dessert?"

"Baked ziti," Alex interrupted. She hoped that would make her dad happy.

Mrs. Russo looked over at Alex. She knew how hard her daughter was trying. She patted her husband on the arm. "Ooh, Jerry," she said. "You *really* love ziti."

Mr. Russo huffed. "I don't think you heard me. I'm trying to cut down on my fruit." When he saw the confused expressions on his family's faces, he explained. "Yes, a tomato is a fruit!" He got up from the table, grabbed his plate, and stormed outside. "I'm going to finish my breakfast for dinner on the terrace."

Alex stood up. "I'll come with you," she called.

"Alone," her dad replied, closing the door behind him.

Alex sat down and tried to salvage what was left of her dignity. "Right, because you don't want me to catch a cold. Thanks, Dad," she said, trying to sound upbeat.

Her mom gave her a smile of encouragement.

Max suddenly piped up. "I know it's all tense and everything, so, I don't have to take a bath tonight, right?" he asked, looking up at his mother for approval.

All he got was a stern look from his mom telling him that was definitely not going to be the case.

After everyone had gone to bed, Justin quietly opened Alex's bedroom door and slipped into her room. It was dark, so he tiptoed carefully. "Alex . . . Alex . . . Alex . . ." he whispered.

Alex tossed and turned, beginning to wake up from a deep sleep.

Just then, Justin bumped into a night table and grunted. Alex sprang up in her bed.

"You scared me!" she exclaimed.

"Shhhhh," Justin hushed her.

Alex smiled. "Oh, I get it," she said, rolling over to switch on the lamp at the side of her bed. "We're pulling a prank on Max like he and I do to you sometimes."

"You guys play pranks on me?" Justin asked, surprised.

"Never mind," Alex told him. "What are you doing in here?"

"Our dinner plan didn't work," he noted.

"I know," Alex grumbled. "And thanks for waking me up to remind me. Good night." She turned off the light and flopped back down in bed.

"Look, flying lessons weren't that easy for me either," he confessed. He flipped the light back on.

"Really?" Alex asked.

"And I'm guessing he's even more intense with Daddy's little princess," Justin went on.

"Yeah, well, Daddy's little princess just got kicked out of the castle," Alex commented. She moved over to the edge of her bed, closer to Justin. "So, whatcha got?"

Justin had a plan. And he knew it was a good one. He smiled. "He only sees you as his little girl. You've got to show him that you're more than that. I'll teach you how to fly, so that way when you go with him next, he'll see how ready you are."

"That's a really good idea," Alex responded. She was impressed.

"Yep," Justin replied. "That's the *J Man's* plan."

"Who?" Alex asked, confused.

"Me," he said, pointing to himself.

Why couldn't everyone figure that out? he wondered. He shook his head and went on to explain. "My name's Justin," he explained. "J is the first letter. It's not that hard!"

Alex rolled her eyes. Her brother could be so weird sometimes. Then she thought for a moment about his plan. "Wait, what's in it for you?"

"You're my little sister. Why's there always

got to be something in it for me?" Justin scoffed.

"*Because* I'm your little sister," Alex replied knowingly.

"And I guess, one day, if you'd like to do something nice for me, then that'd be great," Justin told her.

"Okay, let's go!" Alex exclaimed, leaping out of bed. She stopped at the door and looked back at her big brother. "Wait. I'm going to do something nice for you right now."

"What?" Justin asked.

"Don't use your toothpaste tomorrow morning," Alex advised.

"Why not?" Justin asked.

"It's not toothpaste," Alex said with a laugh as she rushed out the door.

# Chapter Six

It was a beautiful night for flying. The visibility was perfect, and the air traffic was light. The two siblings glided over the Manhattan skyline. Justin sat next to Alex, carefully coaching her through the maneuvers.

"Easy, now . . . easy, now," Justin said encouragingly. "There you go. That's how you make a left turn."

"Wow. With you it's easy," Alex commented

as she held onto the front of the carpet. "Curl left, lean right, go left," she repeated. Even though her father gave the same directions, when the words weren't being shouted at her it was much easier to follow the instructions. She was really flying the carpet!

"I know," Justin said. He had already experienced his dad's intense teaching style. "Now, let's try a right turn." Alex veered the carpet toward the left. "That was good," he said slowly, smiling at his sister's inability to differentiate between left and right. "Now, your other right." When Alex leaned in to the right, the carpet followed smoothly. "There you go!"

"I can *totally* do this," Alex declared. She smiled proudly.

"I knew you could," Justin replied. "And now, you'll be able to show Dad you can."

At that moment, a traffic light appeared in front of them. The light was red.

"Whoa, slow down, slow down!" Justin

commanded. He pointed to the light.

Alex slowed the carpet to a stop. As they waited for the light to change, a flock of wild geese flew by. Just when they thought it was safe to proceed again, a stray bird flew across their path. Alex turned to face Justin.

"That was *so* cool," she said with a smile.

"Be glad it wasn't a hot-air balloon," Justin said with a sigh. "They take forever." He looked down and pointed. "Oh, look, we're flying over Shea Stadium."

Suddenly, a baseball appeared and was heading right toward them! Alex screamed.

"I got it! I got it!" Justin called. The ball hit Justin right on the head. He moaned, rubbing the spot where the ball had just flown into him.

"Yeah, you got it," Alex joked.

Justin brought Alex's attention back to the flying lesson. "Hey, are you ready for something *really* hard?" Justin challenged.

"Like what?" Alex said. Now that she had gotten the hang of flying she was up for trying more stunts.

"The loop de loop!" Justin exclaimed.

"Bring it!" Alex cheered, anxious to show off her new flying abilities.

Immediately, they started spiraling and then flipped completely upside down. "Whoa!" they both yelled.

Safely back on the ground and at their apartment, Alex and Justin rolled up the carpet on the terrace and then quietly slipped inside the house.

"That was so much fun," Alex said. "Thanks, *J Man*."

"Who?" Justin looked puzzled. Then he realized that Alex was referring to him. "Oh, me," he said, pleased that someone remembered his new nickname. "You're welcome. Now, when Dad takes you on your lesson, you'll already know what you're doing."

"Okay, but if he starts yelling 'Up is up and down is down,' I'm going to say something," Alex warned.

Justin gave her a stern look.

"Okay, but I can still think it," Alex said with a shrug.

"Good," Justin said, smiling.

"So, how's your man room?" Alex said as she quietly carried the carpet upstairs.

"Oh, I love it," Justin quickly replied, creeping up the stairs behind her. "It's so great. I sleep like a baby in there."

But in his head, Justin was reliving the scene from the night before. He couldn't fall asleep in his newly decorated room. It was a terror zone! The animal head, the Tears of Blood poster, and the creepy tiki mask were all freaking him out! He had to get rid of this stuff somehow. But he wasn't going to let anyone know why. He'd have to handle the disposal of his new things very carefully. After all, he had made such a fuss about wanting all of these things so he could man up his room. he couldn't let anyone find out that the *J Man* was secretly scared of them!

# Chapter Seven

The next day, Mrs. Russo was sweeping the floor in the Waverly Sub Station. A real New York subway car was part of the décor and made for a very cool place to sit and have lunch or dinner. It was a bright and colorful eatery that was often crowded with customers.

Suddenly, Max ran in from the kitchen.

"Mom! Mom! Guess what Justin gave me?" he said excitedly as he rushed over, holding the boar head in his hands.

When Mrs. Russo saw what Max was holding, she looked over at Justin, who was busy clearing a table of dirty dishes. "Yeah, well, it's a little too babyish for me," he said casually. "'Cause the *J Man* don't do stuffed animals."

"That thing is going right back outside," Mrs. Russo ordered. She couldn't bear to look at it any longer.

Justin called over to his mother. "Hey Mom, are, uh, Dad and Alex back yet?" changing the subject.

Carrying her broom over to the counter, she leaned in and whispered to Justin. "No. And it's been over an hour," she said. She looked around to make sure no one around her was listening. "If they're not back in ten minutes, I want you to go down to the basement and get that broom and go looking for them."

Max suddenly sprang up behind them. "There's a magic flying broom?" he asked.

Trying to cover up what she had just said,

Mrs. Russo waved her hand. "No! I sweep when I'm nervous. And I have a special broom for it." She looked down at the broom in her hand. "That's not this one."

Alex and her dad strolled down the crowded street near the Waverly Sub Station after their day of flying had ended.

"It was fun," he said, smiling over at Alex.

"Dad, you were great," Alex told him. "You're such a good teacher. And didn't I catch on?"

"You know, I've got to say, honey, I'm impressed," her father commented. "You did great."

"Thanks," Alex replied. "And I'm sorry about the last time. I should've listened better."

"No, you know, it wasn't about listening at all. I didn't want to teach you because I didn't want you to grow up," he confessed. "You're my little girl."

Alex smiled and looked up at her dad. "I'll always be your little girl."

Shaking his head, her father knew better. "No, you won't," he said. "Look, you're going to start taking on more grown-up responsibilities, and I have to let you."

"Oh, I don't want to be a grown-up," Alex protested. "I just want to fly. Well, actually I wouldn't mind a credit card, too. You know, so I can stop asking you for money."

Her dad sighed. His three kids definitely kept him busy.

"Oh, I'm so glad you're home!" Mrs. Russo exclaimed as she spotted her husband and daughter walking through the door. She ran up to them and gave them both big hugs. Alex then walked over to where Justin was standing, while Mrs. Russo turned to her husband. "Honey, how'd it go?" she asked.

"She did great," Mr. Russo said proudly. "She listened to me. She's really getting the hang of it." He motioned over to where Justin was standing. "I hate to say it, but she did a little better than Justin," he said quietly.

Overhearing his parents' conversation, Justin leaned over and whispered to Alex. "Yep, you did better than me." He smiled and winked at her.

Mr. Russo walked over to them. "With a couple more lessons," he said to Alex, "you'll be ready to get your carpet license and then you can fly anywhere, including to the store to pick up some pudding for me. Which we never seem to have enough of," he joked.

Alex jumped off the stool and gave her dad a hug and a kiss. "Oh, thanks, Daddy!" she cried as she raced out the door.

"Sure, sweetie," he said to Alex. Then he sat down at the counter. He motioned to Justin. "I don't know what you did, but thanks."

"I didn't do anything," Justin said nervously.

"Really?" his dad asked. "I was watching

the Mets game the other day, and there was a fly ball that went up and never came down. You want to tell me something about that?" He eyed Justin suspiciously.

"Ah . . ." Justin said, attempting to make a fast getaway. He tried to exit through the kitchen door but accidentally backed into the wall instead. He chuckled, turned, and walked through the swinging door before his dad could say anything more. He clearly didn't have the same effect on his dad as Alex when it came to being charming. But he was glad that he was able to help Alex out. And now she owed her big brother. For now, that was enough for the *J Man*.

PART
TWO

# Chapter One

It was Tuesday, and a magic lesson was being held in the Russos' basement. Every Tuesday and Thursday after school, Alex, Max, and Justin gathered in the lair for magic lessons taught by their dad. It was a pretty cool place to hang out and learn about magic. The room had a long desk with three stools for the three Russo wizards in training and a sitting area with comfy couches and chairs.

Mr. Russo was at his lecture stand, explaining the lesson of the day. Justin stood in front of a small cage next to the lecture stand. After his dad finished speaking, Justin pointed his magic wand at a white bunny in the cage. *"Edgebono utoosis,"* he chanted. Suddenly, there were two bunnies! He flipped the wand around in his hand, pleased with himself, and headed back to his seat.

"Good. Thank you, Justin," Mr. Russo said. "That is how you execute the duplication spell properly." He pointed to one of the rabbits in the cage. "Real rabbit. Duplicate, uh, duplicate rabbit, real." Actually, he couldn't tell which one was the real rabbit. "It's . . . anyway, there are two now," he said in frustration.

Mr. Russo tapped the board next to his lecture stand. On the board were written his three rules for casting spells: CONCENTRATE, FOCUS, CLEAR MIND. "Remember," he said to his students, "As with any spell, if you don't concentrate, it doesn't come out exactly right."

At that moment, one of the rabbits started to bark like a dog. Alex, who was lounging on one of the couches, looked up. She had been text messaging a friend from her cell phone. "Oh, that's cool!" she exclaimed. "I've always wanted a guard rabbit. You know, scare off the mailman."

Justin shrugged his shoulders. "I was thinking about dogs when I cast the spell."

"Now," Mr. Russo continued, "are there any questions about the spell?"

Suddenly, Alex jumped up from the couch, interrupting the lesson. "The Crazy Ten-Minute Sale!" she shouted, as she got a news flash from her phone.

"The Crazy *what*?" her dad asked in an annoyed tone. He hated when class was disrupted.

Rushing over to her father, Alex let him in

on the news. "Every year this cool clothing store, Suburban Outfitters, has this crazy sale for ten minutes, where they practically give stuff away and . . ."

Her dad held up his hand and then picked up a remote control. He pointed it right at Alex. "Bee-boop," he said.

Alex looked at her dad in confusion. "What are you doing?" she asked.

"Uh, fast-forwarding to the part where this sale is more important than the magic lesson," Mr. Russo said slowly.

"Well, Gigi's gonna be there," Alex told him.

"Who's Gigi?" her dad asked.

Alex folded her arms across her chest. "Don't you remember? My enemy since kindergarten, when she spilled juice on my mat during nap time and told everyone I had an *accident.*"

Mr. Russo leaned forward on his lecture

stand, pretending to be interested in her story. "This is fascinating. Tell me more," he said sarcastically.

"Well," Alex continued, ignoring her father's sarcasm, "I'm sick of Gigi! She's always rubbing stuff in my face." She knew her father's patience was about to run out so she cut her speech short. "The point is, I'm tired of her always showing me up at school. Can I please skip class on Thursday to go to the sale?"

"Let's roll the answer dice. Shall we?" Mr. Russo said, straightening up. He picked up a pretend pair of dice and blew on his hand before pretending to roll them. "No," he said sternly. He put his arm around Alex and escorted her to a stool at the table between her brothers. "Come on."

"But Dad . . ." Alex whined.

"But nothing," her father said firmly. "Look, you have wizard training on Tuesdays and Thursdays, and you're not ditching."

"You're right, you're right. I'm sorry," Alex said sweetly. "I'm gonna totally focus on the magic." She sat down in her seat and then raised her hand. "I have a question about the spell."

Smiling, Mr. Russo looked at his daughter. "Thank you," he said. He was glad to hear that she was again focusing on the magic lesson.

"How do I use it to get cool clothes before Gigi?" she asked.

Her father tried not to lose patience as he gave Alex a long, hard stare. She definitely had a one-track mind, he thought.

Justin watched his father stare at Alex. It didn't seem like their dad was in the mood to talk about shopping anymore, but clearly Alex wasn't ready to drop the subject. How was Alex going to pull this move off? Their dad took their magic lessons very seriously. But maybe, just maybe, Alex would get her way.

She always had a knack for getting things to work out exactly the way she wanted them to. Especially when it came to shopping. Shopping was one of Alex's favorite activities and she *never* missed a sale. And it was her chance to finally get revenge on Gigi. This was going to be interesting, Justin thought. *Very* interesting.

# Chapter Two

At school the next morning, Alex was standing at her locker before classes began when her best friend Harper Evans came running up to her.

"Are you as excited about the Crazy Ten-Minute Sale as I am?" Harper squealed, clutching her notebook to her chest. Alex looked at Harper and screamed with excitement.

After she calmed down, she turned to

Harper with a serious expression on her face. "I can't go," she admitted, shaking her head sadly.

"But I drew up a game plan so that we can get into the store before Gigi!" Harper insisted. "Do you remember that one-of-a-kind jacket in the window you've been wanting? It's going to be in the sale."

"It all sounds good, but I can't go," Alex said. "It's on Thursday. I have a family commitment." Harper didn't know about the Russos' magic lessons, but she did know that Alex had plans with her family every Tuesday and Thursday after school.

"Do you also have a commitment to letting Gigi run all over you for the rest of your life?" Harper asked.

Alex sighed. Just then, she spotted Gigi and her two wannabe clones walking down the hall. "Great," she commented. "Here she comes with her copycat crew." Alex slammed her locker door shut and turned to Harper, rolling her eyes.

Gigi and her two friends strutted down the hallway. They headed straight over to Alex and Harper.

"*Bonjour*, Alex," Gigi said. Then she looked Harper up and down. "*Bonjour*, Alex's friend."

Harper didn't notice the snotty look on Gigi's face. She was too busy staring at Gigi's feet. "Nice shoes!" she exclaimed. Alex shot her an icy look. Harper quickly copped a sassy attitude. "I mean, I don't care about you *or* your shoes."

Flipping her hair, Gigi sighed. "Yeah, I've had these shoes for about a week. Oh, I mean, I'd give them to you, but I already promised them to another charity."

"No, you should keep them," Alex snapped. "It goes so well with your eyebrow."

"Well, at least I don't have man hands," Gigi

countered. "I mean, how do you get those meat stubs through your sleeves?"

Alex's face burned with embarrassment. Harper stepped in, gesturing at Gigi's two sidekicks. "What happened to *you* two?" Harper asked. The girls each had bandages on their noses. "Pick your noses so hard they fell off?"

"They got nose jobs," Gigi explained.

"When they heal, they'll be just like Gigi's," Gigi's friend announced proudly.

Alex looked at Gigi in amusement. "When's Gigi's gonna heal?"

"People *always* take shots at the trend-setter," Gigi told her haughtily. "And by the way, I saw you looking at that jacket at Suburban Outfitters, and good for you for knowing you need a new one."

Gigi's friends laughed loudly and then they both moaned in pain. Laughing made their noses hurt.

"But it's mine," Gigi continued. "And it'll look so much better on *me*."

"Not if I get it first," Alex challenged.

"Well, good luck finding it," Gigi taunted. "Because I already went down there and hid it."

"Hey, that's not in the spirit of the Crazy Ten-Minute Sale!" Harper cried.

"Yeah, whatever," Gigi said, dismissing her. Then she turned to her friends. "Come on, girls. Time to change your gauze." Before she turned to leave, Gigi grabbed the bottle of juice that one of her friends was holding and poured some on the floor in front of Alex. "Look!" she shouted. "Alex had an accident again!"

Gigi and her friends laughed—and so did everyone else around them who overheard the joke.

"Gigi, this is silly," Alex said, trying to appeal to her. "How long is this gonna go on? We've been with fighting each other forever."

"Fighting? Really?" Gigi asked. "Let's see. I've won, like, three hundred times and you've won none. So it's not really a fight." She turned and left Alex standing there, speechless.

Harper looked over at Alex. "She has won an awful lot," she agreed.

"That's it! We're going to that sale, and I'm going to show her up," Alex declared.

"But I thought you had a family commitment," Harper said.

"I'll work it out with my parents," Alex assured her.

"Sure," Harper said. "They're pretty understanding."

Alex smiled at her friend. "No, I'm just really sneaky," she said with a grin.

At the Waverly Sub Station, the restaurant the family owned that was downstairs from their apartment, Mrs. Russo was busy making sandwiches when her husband walked into the kitchen.

"Honey?" he called.

Absorbed in what she was doing, Mrs. Russo didn't look up.

Mr. Russo had something on his mind, and he needed her undivided attention. He tried again. "Honey?" he asked, a little louder this time.

"Hmm?" she replied, still focusing on the sandwiches.

He gently pulled her away from her work. "Listen. I need you to back me up on this. I told Alex she couldn't miss wizard class to go to some crazy sale on Thursday."

"Okay," Mrs. Russo replied, but then she thought about what her husband had just told her. "Wait. Do you mean the Crazy Ten-Minute Sale?"

"That's the one," Justin chimed in. He was

busy doing the dishes but had overheard his parents' conversation.

Mrs. Russo gasped. "Thank you for reminding me. I almost forgot!" she exclaimed.

"Well, it doesn't sound like you're gonna back me up on this," Mr. Russo grumbled.

Putting her arm on his shoulder, she said, "Don't worry, I am." Then she paused. "Who's not allowed to go again?"

"Alex," Mr. Russo repeated, hoping that his wife would hold to her end of the deal.

"Right," Mrs. Russo said, nodding.

Just then, Max barged into the kitchen. "Wizard mail's here!" he announced.

Justin rushed over to Max. "Oh, *Wizards' Weekly*! Let's see if they printed my letter to the editor!" He grabbed the magazine.

"Ugh!" Max cried as he looked through the mail. "My wand didn't show up." He sulked. "I need my magic wand so I don't have to learn spells anymore."

Hearing Max complain, his dad walked over to him. "Max, you're always going to need to know spells." He tried to explain. "Look, if I give you a bike, that doesn't mean you know how to ride it."

"Awesome!" Max exclaimed. "I'm getting a bike?"

Mr. Russo shook his head. "Look, I know how excited you are about getting your first wand. So, until it comes, how about using old Black Licorice, here?" He took out an old-fashioned black wand from his pocket.

"Yeah, that looks like something you get out of a cereal box," Max told him, not very impressed. If his dad was trying to make him feel better, giving him his old wand was not going to lift his spirits.

"Come on! This is a seventy-seven Wand-warp Featherlight. They don't even make these anymore!" his dad exclaimed.

Max looked at it and rolled his eyes. "I

can see why," he mumbled.

"Look, if you're not gonna take care of it, then I'm not going to give it to you," his dad huffed. He looked at the wand lovingly. "It has tremendous sentimental value. This is the wand that helped me get the goblins out of the basement when I was your age. And it's a tremendous back-scratcher. See?" He scratched his back with the tip of the wand.

"Cool," Max said, though he really wasn't that impressed.

Mr. Russo shrugged. "It's a little dinged up, but . . ."

Mrs. Russo leaned in to take a look at it. "You can see where I filled it in with black nail polish," she said, pointing out the patched spots.

Mr. Russo stood back to admire it. "There are a lot of great memories wrapped up in this wand," he bragged.

"And a lot of stories I'm tired of hearing,"

Mrs. Russo commented as she hurried out of the kitchen.

Justin and Max laughed. When their dad gave them a disapproving look, Justin put up his hands innocently. "She said it, we didn't," he said, still chuckling.

Max grabbed the wand out of his dad's hand and ran out of the kitchen. His dad's old wand was better than no wand!

# Chapter Three

On Thursday afternoon, Alex was in the lair waiting for the magic lesson to begin. She was standing in front of the mirror, smoothing out a few wrinkles in her blue shirt. "How do I look?" she asked Max.

Not looking up from his handheld video game, Max asked, "Why?"

"Because I'm going to duplicate myself and if I look ugly, I don't want to look twice as ugly," Alex explained.

"What are you talking about?" Max asked, looking up.

"I'm talking about taking Gigi down, and it's gonna take more than one of me to do it," she said. She waved her magic wand over her head and chanted, *"Edgebono utoosis."* Suddenly, there were two Alexes in the room!

"Now *that's* cool!" Max exclaimed, impressed to see that the spell worked.

Justin walked into the basement and greeted his siblings. "Afternoon, Alex. Other Alex. You're both clearly up to no good."

"Max, just help me get me ready so it looks like I'm here so I can leave," Alex pleaded, ignoring Justin. She stopped and looked at the clone that she created. "Wow, I did a great job," she said, nodding her head in approval.

Just then, the clone lifted her head and barked like a dog!

"Ugh!" Alex shouted. She turned to glare at Justin. "I was thinking about your stupid barking rabbit. Bad girl," Alex scolded her clone, shaking her finger at her. "No barking, just pout."

"Yeah, I don't see how this could possibly go wrong," Justin said sarcastically. He looked over at Alex and her clone.

"It'll be fine," Alex said. "The real me is upset with Dad, which means I pout and give him the silent treatment."

"Yeah, but for how long?" Justin asked.

"Well, this clone has to pout for the Ten-Minute Sale plus travel time, which shouldn't be a problem because my pout record is like, four days," she said proudly.

Suddenly, Alex's cell phone rang. "Hello?" she answered.

It was Harper, who was already standing outside of Suburban Outfitters. "Alex," she said impatiently, "are you sneaking away or not? The doors are going to open any minute and Gigi's already in the front!"

"How did she get up front?" Alex asked Harper.

"I don't know, but she's telling everybody you shop in preteen," Harper reported. "Which I said wasn't a slam, because a lot of their stuff is really, really cute. Like my sunflower top that goes with my rainbow socks."

"I'll be right there," Alex said. Then she thought about what Harper had just said. "Wait, you're not wearing that, are you?"

Harper glanced down at her outfit. "No," she lied as she pulled her sweatshirt closed, hiding her shirt.

Alex quickly hung up the phone and turned to her brothers.

Justin was staring at her in disbelief. "You *really* think Dad will be fooled with this thing sitting here with that glassy look in its eye, totally disconnected during class?" he asked. Then he considered the plan and how Alex usually was during wizard training. "Wow, you're right. This could work."

"What if Dad asks you to change seats or something?" Max asked, worried that he'd have to move Alex's clone from the chair in the middle of the room to the stool. How was he going to do that?

"I don't know, cover for me," Alex said with a huff. She had to get to the store quickly.

Max scoffed. "Why would I cover for you?" he asked.

"Because I'll buy you a brand-new pair of sneakers," Alex told him as she headed toward the door.

"Sold!" Max cheered.

"I'm off to the sale, and Mom and Dad know nothing about that, right?" Alex asked slyly.

Max mimed zipping his lips shut. "I'm a size five," he called after her.

After she left, Justin looked over at Max.

"That's your price?" he asked. "A new pair of sneakers?"

"Apparently," Max replied. "But the joke's on her. I'm gonna get some new sneakers for doing nothing."

"What are you gonna do when she falls over and you have to cover for her with Dad?" Justin said, pointing to the clone of Alex sitting in the chair.

"That will never happen," Max said confidently.

"You're right," Justin said mischievously. "It'll never happen." Then he walked over and tapped the clone on the shoulder so that it toppled over in a heap on the floor.

Max looked horrified. This was not going to make Alex happy!

Meanwhile, back at Surburban Outfitters, there was a glitch in Alex's plan. While Harper was waiting for Alex to show up, another Russo arrived.

"Hi, Harper!" Mrs. Russo exclaimed, greeting her daughter's best friend.

"Hi, Alex's mom," Harper responded politely. Then she realized what this meant. Alex and her mom were at the very same place, when Alex was supposed to be at home! "Oh, my gosh! Alex's mom!" she cried.

"I know it's weird for a grown-up to be here," Mrs. Russo said, reacting to Harper's surprised look. "But since Alex couldn't come, I'm going to get something for her." She tried to act cool. "Well, this will be fun. It's a chance for you and me to spend some time together." She did a little dance move. "You know, chill!"

Harper had to think about how she was going to distract Mrs. Russo, and fast! Alex was going to be there any minute. This shopping adventure had taken a totally wrong turn. Harper would have to act quickly if this were all going to work out.

# Chapter Four

By the time Alex arrived at Suburban Outfitters, there was a large crowd gathered outside the store. "Excuse me," Alex said, pushing her way through everyone. She was looking for Harper. She spotted her bright rainbow socks and sighed gratefully. "There you are!"

"How did you find me with all these people?" Harper asked in amazement.

"I saw your rainbow socks from down the block," Alex said, smiling. "Sorry I'm late. It took a while to ditch the family."

Harper looked around nervously at the crowd. "Well, you didn't do a very good job," she said. "Your mom's here!"

"What?" Alex shrieked. Her brilliant plan was about to be ruined!

Harper grinned reassuringly. "Relax," she said. "I sent her down the block to find some Tappucinos."

"There's no such thing as a Tappucino," Alex pointed out.

Harper smiled and nodded her head slowly. "I know," she said with a sly grin.

"Wow, I'm impressed," Alex commented. "You're becoming more like me every day."

The crowd was inching closer to the door, and Alex knew it was time to spring into action. "Okay, move!" she called over her shoulder, as she pushed her way up to the front of the line. "Excuse me. Sorry," she said as she worked her way to the door. When she got to the front, Alex fell forward onto a very aggressive shopper. "Excuse me," Alex said. Then she realized who was standing next to her. "Nice try, Gigi. But it looks like I got in the front of the line, too."

With her face pressed up against the store's front door, Gigi mumbled, "Well, I know where the jacket is and you don't."

"What's that?" Alex asked. "You're looking for a racket? Well, I'm looking for a jacket. And I'm gonna get it before you do." Alex noticed an older woman standing next to Gigi. She was holding a plastic cup of iced tea. Alex looked at Gigi and rolled her eyes. "I can't believe you brought your grandma here. She's not gonna help you get in first."

"She's not my grandma," Gigi snipped. "I found her at the park. She's here to block."

Just then, the door opened and the crowd

pushed their way through. Alex was relieved to finally get into the store.

Gigi ran over to a small table and started to look for the jacket that she thought she had so cleverly hid. "Where is it?" she cried. "It was right here!"

Just then, she spotted a store manager who was walking by. "Excuse me," she said sweetly. "There was a huge pile of clothes right there. Where is it?"

"Oh, we completely rearranged the store for the sale, because a lot of people sneak in early and hide stuff," the woman reported. "It's not really in the spirit of the Crazy Ten-Minute Sale."

Overhearing the conversation, Alex couldn't contain herself. "Ha! It's anybody's jacket now!" She raced off, with Gigi following closely behind her. The race to find the jacket was officially on!

At that moment, Mrs. Russo came rushing

into the store, holding a tray with two tall cups. "Harper!" she called.

Harper panicked and grabbed a large orange bag that was on the table to hide under.

"Harper?" Mrs. Russo called out again, searching the crowd. She was so excited about finally finding the drinks that she didn't seem bothered about not finding Harper right away. "I found our Tappucinos! It's steamed milk and tap water," she said, laughing.

Mrs. Russo walked right by Harper, searching the shop for her sale buddy.

Whew, thought Harper. She wondered how long she'd be able to dodge Mrs. Russo and keep Alex out of sight. This was the craziest sale ever!

Back in the lair, Max was struggling with the clone that Alex had created of herself. He couldn't pick it up off the floor.

"Oh, she's too heavy," he said with a moan.

He looked over at Justin. "Can you give me a hand?"

"Why don't you use Dad's wand to help move her?" Justin said from his seat. He didn't want to help Max, as he was trying to stay out of this plan. He *knew* it was going to be trouble.

Max fell back on the couch, exhausted. "I can't find it," he whined.

Just then, Max heard a loud crack!

Justin looked over at his younger brother.

"No! No, no, no!" Max screamed, jumping up and down. He pulled the broken wand out of his back pocket and stared at it. "Dad's gonna wig out. You know, if I wasn't getting new sneakers, I'd be really freaked out."

"Oh, I'd be really freaked out anyway," Justin quipped.

Max groaned as he tried to move the clone. It kept falling over on the floor. Finally, Max thought he had gotten it to sit upright in the chair. But like a rag doll, it fell forward on top of him.

Just then, Mr. Russo walked into the lair with the wizard mail and threw it on the chair. He was ready to begin the day's lesson. But he paused when he looked up and saw who he *thought* was Alex slumped over Max in a slow-dancing position.

"What are you doing?" he asked.

Quickly, Max spun the clone around in a fancy ballroom turn. "Dancing. With my sister. P-Practicing for that new reality show, *Dancing with My Sister*," Max stammered as he danced the body over to Alex's seat. He gently placed it down. Alex's clone sat with its head hanging down.

Mr. Russo rolled his eyes. "Okay, guys," he said, walking over to the table where Justin, Max, and Alex's clone were sitting. "Before we get started today, I just want to point out the good example set by your sister." He stopped and stood by the duplicate Alex. "She really wanted to go shopping, but instead she's right here, ready to learn."

Justin didn't look up. "I think we're all gonna learn something real soon," he mumbled.

"Alex, I'm very proud of you," Mr. Russo gushed. "So proud, I'm gonna give you permission to miss today's lesson and go to that sale. So go ahead and have fun." He grinned and waited for Alex to jump up and give him a hug. When she didn't move, he gave the clone a nudge. "Seriously. Go!"

Max knew this was going to be trouble. "Uh-oh," he muttered under his breath.

"Oh," Mr. Russo said with a laugh. "I get it. You need money." He reached into his pocket and took out some cash. "I'm sorry." He handed the money to Alex's clone. "Go ahead, take it."

Justin couldn't believe the charade was

still going on! "Yeah, Alex. Take it," he said, waiting to see how long it would take for his father to catch on.

Suddenly, Mr. Russo realized that Alex still wasn't moving. He suddenly realized what was going on. He took a step back and glared at his sons. "Alex used the duplication spell and went to the Crazy Ten-Minute Sale!" he exclaimed loudly.

"Wow, it looks like she did," Max said with as much innocence as he could muster. "This is way worse than me breaking your wand. Right?"

Mr. Russo was furious! It was hard to tell which situation—the broken wand or the clone—was making him angrier. He ran out of the room.

Justin walked over to the chair to look through the wizard mail. "That would've been a good time to tell him I broke his new drill last week," he commented.

"You broke his drill?" Max asked.

"I think so," Justin admitted. "I'll find out when I put the pieces back together."

Max opened a box with his name on it. "Check it out!" he cried. "My new eWand!" Instantly, he was in a much better mood.

"Oh, an eWand," Justin said, grabbing it. He held up a cord at the end. "That strap is for safety."

"Good point," Max said as he tore off the strap. "Now that we've got *safety* out of the way, let's rock." He waved the wand in the air, and it flew out of his hands. "Whoa, slippery!"

"Wow, they should make something that attaches to the wand so that doesn't happen," Justin said dryly.

Max rolled his eyes at his brother. Sure, the wand was powerful, but Max would get the hang of it. He loved it! It was even better than the new sneakers, which he was pretty sure he wasn't going to get, considering that his dad was on his way now to get Alex from Suburban Outfitters.

# Chapter Five

Back at the sale, Harper spotted Alex walking toward her. "Alex!" she shrieked. "Hide! Your mom's right behind me!"

"What?" Alex panicked. She quickly dove into a pile of clothes next to her. She didn't want to take any chances of seeing her mom and blowing her cover.

Mrs. Russo finally spotted Harper in the crowded store.

"Harper!" she shouted. "There you are! I

found our Tappucinos. They're surprisingly delicious."

Harper was ready to freak out. She had to act fast! She came up with a good distraction. She bumped into Mrs. Russo's tray so that the beverages spilled all over the floor. It wasn't the best—or the neatest—move, but it seemed to work. "I'm sorry!" she cried. She grabbed Mrs. Russo's shoulders to lead her in the other direction. "Let's go tell a manager."

Just then, the store manager zoomed past them and made an announcement on the intercom. "Eight minutes left in the Crazy Ten-Minute Sale!" she declared.

"Are you kidding me?" Mrs. Russo whined. "I've only got eight minutes to find something for Alex?" She turned to Harper. "What do you think she'd like?"

Harper mumbled, "For you to leave."

"What?" Mrs. Russo said, not hearing what Harper had said.

Harper grabbed a shirt and pushed it toward Alex's mom. "This is your size," she said. "Go try it on." She directed her to the fitting room.

After Mrs. Russo walked away in confusion, Alex popped her head up out of the pile of clothes. "Alex, are you okay?" Harper asked.

Alex jumped up. "I'm fine, I'm fine. Did my mom see me?"

"No," Harper assured her. "I sent her to the dressing room. But this is our chance. Let's get out of here." She tried to push Alex in the direction of the front door of the store.

But Alex stood her ground. "Oh, no. I am *not* leaving without that jacket."

"Harper!" Mrs. Russo called out.

"Oh, I'm going back in," Alex said with a sigh. She dove back into the pile of clothing, hoping that she wouldn't be found.

In the lair, Justin and Max were examining Max's new wand. Since their dad had run off to find Alex, they were trying to figure out what the wand was capable of doing.

"Hey, what else does this thing do?" Max asked. He loved its cool design but wondered about its other features.

Justin looked up from the small scroll of instructions that came with the wand. "Standard magic stuff," Justin reported, still reading. "It, uh, opens portals, disappears objects, levitates things, and . . ." he suddenly glanced up from reading. "Oh, my gosh!"

"What?" Max cried. He leaned in closer to his brother.

"It's an MP3 player!" Justin exclaimed. "It holds a trillion songs!"

"No way," Max said in total disbelief. He couldn't believe his luck!

"Oh, and it says here it has an eMimic feature," Justin said, pointing to the directions. "What's that?"

Max was flipping the wand around in his

hand when the tip started to glow. He tapped the clone of Alex on its face, and the double started to slap her face with her hand! "I think I just found out," he said with a sly smile. The eMimic feature was doing exactly what Max was!

Meanwhile at Suburban Outfitters, the real Alex was standing in the middle of the store. But she wasn't trying on her beloved jacket. She was smacking herself in the face!

Gigi walked over to Alex and gave her an odd look. "Why are you hitting yourself?" she asked. She knew Alex could act strange at times, but this was very bizarre, even for Alex!

"I don't know!" Alex cried. She couldn't stop! She had no control over what she was doing. Not to mention that her face was starting to hurt!

"Oh, I know what you're doing," Gigi said.

"We must be getting close to the jacket. You're trying to distract me!"

Just then, Gigi's two friends came running over.

"Why are you hitting yourself?" one of the girls asked. "You've got problems." She looked at Alex in bewilderment.

Suddenly, Alex had the urge to do the chicken dance. She started doing the silly dance moves—right in the middle of the store!

"Whoa," Gigi commented, backing away from Alex. "What are you doing now?"

Alex tried to act nonchalant. "Uh, what does it look like I'm doing?" she asked. "I'm dancing like a chicken."

"I don't even know why I try to embarrass you," Gigi said with a sigh. "I mean, you're so good at it yourself." She motioned to her friends, and the trio walked away.

Harper suddenly spotted Alex and came

over to see what was going on.

"I don't know what's happening!" Alex cried.

"I do," Harper said calmly. "You're dancing like an Egyptian!" She raised her hands up by her head and mimicked the steps Alex was doing.

Gigi was still watching Alex, and since she never missed an opportunity to humiliate her, she grabbed the intercom microphone and made an announcement. "Hey, everyone," she called. "There's a freak show by the jeans rack!" She smirked as she once again called attention to Alex in an embarrassing situation. Gigi's friends laughed and pointed in Alex's direction.

Hearing the announcement, Harper's smile widened. "Hey, Alex!" she shouted. "I think we caught a break. There's some freak show by the jeans. Let's go look."

Alex sighed. "Harper, *those* are the jeans,"

she said, pointing to the rack behind them. "*I'm* the freak show!"

Back in the Russo's basement, Max was giddy with excitement. He loved the power of his new wand! And he especially loved the way that the clone of Alex was dancing! Little did he know that the real Alex was doing the same thing—all because of him and his wand. He positioned the clone on a stool. Max laughed and waved his wand around, forcing the clone to spin around wildly. He laughed even louder. This is the coolest wand ever, Max thought happily.

In Suburban Outfitters, the real Alex was spinning around like a tornado at warp speed! She grabbed a shirt off a clothing rack, trying to slow down. She bumped into Harper and handed her the shirt.

Harper smiled. "Size seven. Perfect. Thanks,

Alex," she said, not noticing that Alex was now spinning in circles.

"Help me!" Alex pleaded.

Just then, Mr. Russo rushed into the store. He spotted his wife right away. "Theresa!" he shouted. "Where's Alex?"

"She's with you," Mrs. Russo replied, not realizing that Alex was actually in the store.

"No, she's not," he explained. "She cut class. I came down here to look for her." He scanned the store and tried to spot Alex.

"Well, I haven't seen her," Mrs. Russo answered.

Just then, a whirl of blue spun by. Mr. Russo sighed. "I think I just did." It was hard to miss the spinning Alex whiz through the store. "Alex!" he yelled. "Stop spinning wildly out of control and get over here!"

"I can't!" she cried. Her twirling led her to a large bin of clothes. She finally stopped spinning and fell in. *"Ahhhhhhhh!"* she screamed.

"What do you think is going on?" Mrs. Russo asked, turning to her husband.

Mr. Russo took a deep breath. "I think Max got his new wand," he said.

"I found it!" Alex called from the bin. She sat up, holding the prized jacket she had been searching for. "I found the jacket!" Standing in the bin, Alex called over to her nemesis. "Hey, Gigi, guess what's in my meat hands," she taunted.

Gigi ran over and tried to grab the jacket from Alex. "Give me the jacket!" she ordered. "Give it to me!"

"No!" Alex said defiantly. There was no way that she was giving it up now!

As they continued to struggle, the older woman that Alex encountered at the store's entrance walked by, still holding her beverage. Gigi accidentally bumped into her.

"Give me . . ." Gigi was seething. She suddenly felt something dripping down the front of her pants. She gasped in horror. Her jeans were covered in iced tea!

"Well, it looks like the tink*lee* became the tink*ler*," Alex remarked, quite pleased that their roles were now reversed.

Gigi smirked. "Oh, *please*," she said. "Everybody saw her spill that on me."

Gigi's friends stood across from her, staring at her in disgust. The two girls laughed and pointed at her. Gigi was mortified.

"Where are you going?" Gigi yelled at her friends as they turned and walked away. She couldn't believe her friends thought that she had an accident!

"They're gone, Gigi," Alex said, walking over to her. "They left you."

"Okay, maybe you're right," Gigi said defeatedly. "This has been going on for too long."

"No, it hasn't," Alex declared. "I'm just getting good at it. In fact, I think it's time for a little announcement." She turned around and saw her parents standing there. She could tell from the look on their faces that they were really angry. "Okay, I know I'm in trouble. But just, like, one second," she said, holding up her hand. She just had to do one more thing before she left to face her punishment.

Alex ran over to the microphone. "Attention, shoppers," Alex announced. Her parents were trying to pull her toward the door. "Gigi's real name is Gertrude," she managed to say before her parents started to lead her out of the store.

She turned to her parents. "Okay, now I can go." She knew she was totally going to be grounded, but finally getting revenge on Gigi was *so* worth it.

As the Russos' left, the manager sighed. "These sales get crazier and crazier every year," she muttered to herself.

# Chapter Six

"Oh, Alex!" Max called as he saw his sister walk into the lair. "Dad's looking for you."

Justin looked up from his desk to see his dad standing right behind Alex. "And he found you," he commented.

"Did you get your wand today, Max?" Mr. Russo asked.

"Uh . . . yeah," Max replied. He sat up straight in his seat.

"Because whatever you were doing to this

dummy," he said, pointing to the cloned Alex, "was happening to *this* dummy," he added, as he gestured to the real Alex.

Max nodded his head. His dad was now beginning to make sense. "Oh, that's what the *mimic* in eMimic means," he said slowly.

"I told you we should've read the manual!" Justin exclaimed.

Mr. Russo looked over at Max. "Max, you know better than to use magic without my permission," he said sternly.

Max could tell from his father's tone that he was angry. He had to think of a way to get out of this one. "You're right, Dad," he said in agreement. "It was pretty bad what I did. But not as bad as Alex using magic to cut class to go to some sale."

"Yes, Max. Thank you," his father said dryly. "And you and I by no means are done talking about this," he said, directing his attention back to Alex.

"I know," Alex said, anticipating what was coming next. "But before we get into it, I think you should know, I heard Justin broke your drill."

Mr. Russo turned to stare at his older son. "My brand-new drill?" he asked.

"Max broke your wand," Justin spat out.

Mr. Russo took a deep breath. He looked at his three children. He turned to Justin and tried to remain calm. "Did you use magic to break my drill?"

Shaking his head, Justin uttered, "No."

He waved his oldest son out of the room. "You're clear," he ordered. "Go."

He then turned to Max, looking at him with a serious gaze. "Did you use magic to break my wand?" he inquired.

Max shook his head innocently. "No," he said. "I sat on it." He shrugged and looked up at his dad hopefully.

Taking a deep breath, Mr. Russo waved Max

out of the basement. "You're clear. Go," he said.

Alex was the only one left in the room. He turned to her. "And we have a winner!" he proclaimed.

"Dad, I know you're mad, but I can explain," she said. "Gigi has been making me look bad forever, and this was a huge chance to get back at her. So I went for it."

"Ah, revenge," her father said slowly.

"So you do get it?" Alex asked. She was encouraged by the fact that her father didn't seem that angry anymore. Maybe he did understand?

He sat down next to her. "I get it," he said. Then he got up and walked around the room. "Let's look at it, shall we? Was revenge worth missing your wizard training? Was it worth having your brother lie for you or . . . or your best friend lie to your mom down at that store?"

"So, what you're saying is, by getting back

at Gigi, I was really hurting myself," Alex told him, trying to paraphrase what he was saying and get to the end of this conversation quickly.

"No," her father said. Then he nodded. "But I like that better."

"So, since I figured that out," Alex said sweetly, "I should pick my own punishment, right?"

"No," her father replied. "Why don't you take my punishment and duplicate it? You're grounded for one week."

"Does that mean two weeks?" she asked. She had to clarify. Did he really mean *double* the punishment?

"Oh, now it's four!" Mr. Russo declared. He chuckled to himself. "I love this game!" He headed for the door.

The duplicate Alex popped up its head and barked.

Alex gave the clone a dirty look. "Oh, you hush up," she scolded.

This shopping day had *not* gone as expected. Not only was her duplicate spell a complete disaster, she didn't even get the jacket she wanted. But at least she got even with Gigi. And that was greater than any crazy sale!

Later that evening, Alex was downstairs catching up on her homework. Her dad spotted her and was pleased that she seemed to be accepting her punishment.

"So, I'm glad you learned your lesson," he said.

"Me, too," Alex said, looking up at her dad.

"Good," he agreed. He began to shuffle his feet nervously. "Now, um, your mom wants me to take her out dancing, but the big game is on tonight," he confessed.

Alex knew right away what he was going to ask.

"Dad, that sounds like your punishment, not mine," Alex told him, smiling.

"Then you see what I'm getting at?" he said.

Alex knew exactly where this question was going. "Oh, you want me to duplicate you so you can go dancing *and* watch the game."

"A little," Mr. Russo admitted.

Alex gave her dad a mischievous grin. She waved her wand twice and chanted the duplication spell. *"Edgebono utoosis!"*

Suddenly, there were two Mr. Russos standing in the room! Mr. Russo turned to his clone and gave it instructions. "Have her home by eleven," he said.

Alex laughed. But she understood. Having three wizards in the family had to be difficult, but if you couldn't reap the benefits of a little of their magic, what good would they be?

Something magical is on the way!
Look for the next book in the
Wizards of Waverly Place series.

# Haywire

Adapted by Beth Beechwood

Based on the series created by Todd J. Greenwald

Part One is based on the episode, "I Almost Drowned in a Chocolate Fountain,"
Written by Gigi McCreery & Perry Rein

Part Two is based on the episode, "Curb Your Dragon," Written by Gigi McCreery & Perry Rein

Alex Russo hurried down the stairs of Tribeca Prep. She had just spotted her best friend, Harper Evans, and couldn't wait to tell her the news. She approached Harper, waving a piece of paper in the air. "Check it out!" she shouted happily. "I got an F on my Spanish midterm!"

Harper was puzzled. "Why are you so happy about it?" she asked.

Alex smiled. "Because Riley got an F, too. That means he's been paying as much attention to me as I've been to him." She let out a big sigh, as an image of her crush flashed through her head. "Failing Spanish is hard work," she said dramatically.

Again, Harper was confused by her friend's reaction. "How is failing Spanish hard work?"

Alex tried to explain. Sometimes her best friend had trouble catching on to what Alex was trying to tell her. "Every day I show up late so he'll definitely notice me. Then, I 'forget' my textbook, so we have to share one. And finally, I let the teacher catch us passing notes, so she keeps us both after class."

Harper nodded sympathetically. "That *is* hard work. You must be exhausted," she said.

Just then, Riley walked up to them.

"Hey, Alex," Riley said casually. "A bunch

of us are going to this cool restaurant, Medium Rare, on Friday night," he said. "Wanna come?"

Alex pretended to know the restaurant well, even though she had never heard of it before in her life. After all, she *did* live in New York City and she didn't want Riley to think she wasn't hip to the coolest places to hang out. "Oh, sure," she said with a smile. "Medium Rare. I go there all the time."

"But it's new," Riley replied. "Friday's opening night."

Uh-oh, Alex thought. She quickly corrected herself. "Oh, Medium *Rare*," she said, laughing. "I thought you said Medium *Roar*. You know, like, bigger than a kitten, and smaller than a lion, you know—like a cougar. Anyway, it's out by the zoo." She gave Riley a confident smile.

He smiled back and then turned to Harper. "You can come, too," he said politely.

"Well, I might as well," Harper shrugged,

"since my best friend never took me to Medium Roar," she said with a huff. Harper once again missed the whole thing and bought Alex's convoluted story.

After agreeing to meet the girls at the restaurant on Friday night, Riley walked off, leaving them to discuss what had just occurred.

"Look at that," Alex commented. "All those hours I didn't spend on studying totally paid off."

But Harper was barely paying attention. She was distracted by the boy walking toward them. "Oh, no! Here comes your brother," she said to Alex. "I think he's coming over here. Oh, he's so cute. I never know what to say to him."

Though Alex could not, for the life of her, understand the crush Harper had on her older brother, Justin, she tried to help. "Uh, just talk about current events. He *loves* current events," she suggested.

"Hey, guys," Justin said cheerfully.

"Alex failed her Spanish midterm!" Harper blurted out.

Justin looked over at Alex in amusement.

Alex turned to glare at her friend. "Not *that* current!"

Oh, great, Alex thought to herself. If Justin tells Mom and Dad about this, I'm definitely not going to Medium Rare on Friday night!

# Get More of Your Favorite Pop Star!

Includes 8 full-color postcards!

**Poster Book**

POSTER BOOK

From the hit TV series on Disney Channel

**Bonus:**
8 postcards to send to friends!

Keeping Secrets

Face-off

Seeing Green

**Includes 12 posters of the show's stars!**

**Collect all the stories about Hannah Montana!**

**Don't Bet on It**

Sweet Revenge

**Win or Lose**

© Disney

DISNEY PRESS
AN IMPRINT OF DISNEY BOOK GROUP
**www.disneybooks.com**

Available wherever books are sold

# Keep Rockin'!

© Disney

Includes color photos of the stars!

www.disneybooks.com

**Available wherever books are sold**

DISNEY PRESS
AN IMPRINT OF DISNEY BOOK GROUP